and the
Hairy
Scary
Spider

illustrated by

Peter H. Reynolds

CANDLEWICK PRESS

Text copyright © 2020 by Megan McDonald
Illustrations copyright © 2020 by Peter H. Reynolds
Stink® is a registered trademark of Candlewick Press, Inc.

First paperback edition 2021

Library of Congress Catalog Card Number 2020915494
ISBN 978-1-5362-0920-4 (hardcover)
ISBN 978-1-5362-1388-1 (paperback)

21 22 23 24 25 26 TRC 10 9 8 7 6 5 4 3 2 1

Printed in Eagan, MN, USA

This book was typeset in Stone Informal and hand-lettered by the illustrator. The illustrations were created digitally.

Candlewick Press
99 Dover Street
Somerville, Massachusetts 02144

www.candlewick.com

for Richard,
friend to spiders
MM

To my big brother, Andy,
who is famous for his love of spiders
and other creepy-crawly things!
PHR

CONTENTS

Hairy!

Scary!

Be wary!

Stink was on a kick. Stink was on a roll. Stink was in the zone. The paper-folding zone. Stink was cuckoo-crazy for origami.

Fold. Crease. Press. Turn. Flip.

He folded an orange origami fish. He folded a purple origami pinwheel. He folded a red origami ladybug.

Stink could not stop folding. He folded junk mail into a string of sailboats. He folded sticky notes into an army of ants. He even folded candy wrappers. He made a candy-bar dog, a bubble-gum ring, and a lollipop bow tie.

Easy-peasy!

Stink practiced folding Beginner Level origami. One day, he was going to advance to Level Medium.

Then Stink took out his lunch-money

dollar bill. He folded it in half. He folded the corners down. He flipped it over. He folded the bottom up and the sides in. He folded the back legs. He folded the front legs. He made a zigzag fold and ta-da!

His dollar-bill jumping frog was ready to hop.

Stink took the origami frog outside. He pressed the back of the frog. It jumped across the deck. He pressed it again. It leaped across the yard. Again. It leaped into the tall weeds at the corner of the fence.

Stink ran over to get his jumping

frog. Where was it? Stink pushed apart
some tall weeds, when what to his
wondering eye did appear?

Something in the grass. Something
pink!

Was it a flower petal? A jelly bean?
Doughnut sprinkles? An old piece of

pink play clay? Maybe the pink thingy was a rare pink-flamingo mushroom!

Stink peered closer. Wait just a leap-frog second!

The pink thingy moved! The pink thingy was not just one pink thingy. It was several pink hairy things. And the pink hairy things were attached to even bigger, hairier . . . legs!

And the legs were attached to an even bigger, hairier . . . body.

And the body was attached to a giant, hairy . . . head.

And the hairy head had a bazillion and one eyes.

The pink thing in the weeds was a giant . . .

hairy . . .

scary . . .

spider!

Stink had never seen a spider so hairy. He had never seen a spider with so many eyes. Were those fangs?

He had never seen a spider with pink toes!

This was some kind of monster spider. A mutant spider that had escaped from a top-secret super-scientific radioactive lab.

Creature from the Pink Lagoon!

"Run!" Stink yelled to nobody but himself.

He ran. He ran into the house and through the kitchen and down the hall and up the stairs to his room. He slammed the door shut. He pulled a blanket around himself.

Bwaaaa! He shivered. Stink did not, would not, could not, like spiders. He had been meaning to get over his fear of spiders, but he had never gotten around to it.

What was a giant mutant spider doing in his very own backyard anyway?

Frogs? Yes. Toads. Definitely. Snails, slugs, and skinks? You betcha. Backyards would be boring without them.

But spiders made him shiver. Spiders made his skin crawl. Spiders felt like a thousand tiny prickly feet marching up and down his arms and legs.

Stink did not, would not, could not, go back out into the yard. But he had to get his jumping frog back. After all, it was one whole dollar bill!

If only he knew somebody who was

NOT afraid of spiders. *Hmm.*

Eureka! Stink *did* know somebody who was NOT afraid of spiders.

Judy Moody!

His big sister thought wolf spiders were "cute." She was not a Squisher. She was a Saver who set spiders free when they got inside the house. She once held a daddy longlegs in her bare hand.

Spiders had eight legs and about a million eyes. Okay, eight eyes. But in The World According to Stink, eight of anything was too many.

He was not, no way, no how, going back out there alone.

Stink found Judy in her room making a pet rock. "Hey, Judy! Are you up for a scare?"

"Always," said Judy. "What did you have in mind? Telling spooky stories?"

"Scarier," said Stink.

"Looking for a ghost in Grandma Lou's basement?"

"Scarier," said Stink.

"What's scarier than that?" Judy asked.

"A ginormous, hairy, scary, radio-active mutant spider!"

"Cool," said Judy. "Does it glow in the dark?" Judy tickled Stink's arm

with a feather. *"The itsy-bitsy spider went up—"*

Stink shook her off. "There is nothing itsy-bitsy about this spider. It has a million furry legs and a billion buggy eyes and venom-dripping fangs. It even has pink toes."

"There's no such thing as a pink-toed spider," said Judy. "First of all, spiders don't have toenails. Second of all, spiders do not wear pink."

"You gotta see this thing. Up close and for reals."

"No thanks." She glued a googly eye onto the rock.

"Are you telling me that you, Judy Moody, have a chance to lay eyes on the world's hairiest, scariest spider—I mean, we're talking museum-quality spider here—but you would rather sit here and play with a rock?"

"Yep."

"I'm telling you, this thing is gargantuan. It's tarantulan!"

"Tarantula? Why didn't you say so? Tarantulas are the coolest."

"I double-dog-pink-toe dare you to come see the hairiest, scariest spider ever."

Judy put down her pet rock. "Challenge accepted!"

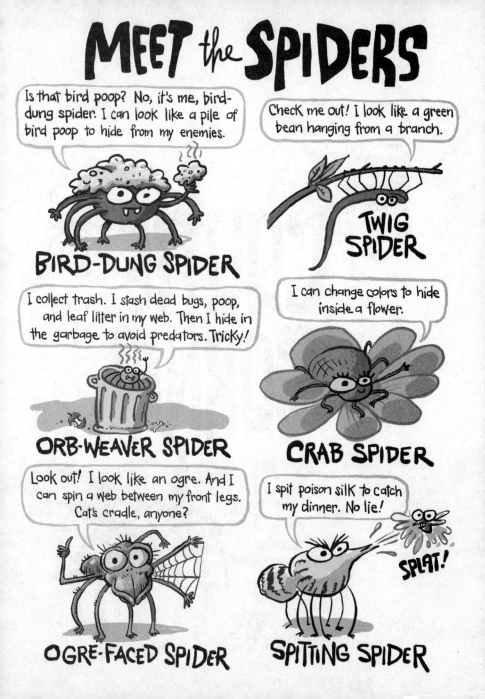

Stink pulled Judy into the way-back corner of the yard. He pointed to the tall weeds. "That's right where it is. Cootie Corner."

"Cootie Corner?" asked Judy.

"I just named it that, because it has cooties now. Big, fat spider cooties."

Judy pawed through the tall grass. "There's nothing here, Stink."

"Nothing big and hairy?" said Stink.

"Nope."

"How about something with a hundred pink toes?" said Stink.

"Nope," said Judy. "Maybe it was just a leaf. Or a piece of bark or something. Besides, tarantulas don't live around here anyway."

"Where do they live?"

"I think they live in the desert. Like in South America. Or Texas."

"This one lives in Virginia," said Stink. "It was right here. I swear."

"I'm going back inside," said Judy.

"But we didn't find my dollar-bill frog!" called Stink, running after her.

Stink called his friend Sophie of the

Elves. Sophie came right over. Stink led her straight to Cootie Corner. But the spider was not there. No tarantula. Nothing. So Sophie went home.

Stink called his friend Webster Gomez. Webster came right over. Stink led him straight to Cootie Corner. But the spider was not there. No tarantula. Nada.

"It was here, honest," said Stink. "And guess what. It had pink toes."

"I believe you," said Webster. "My cousin Marcos has a red-knee tarantula. He knows about all kinds of tarantulas. He told me all about pink-toe tarantulas. They live in trees instead of on the ground, and they're nocturnal. They come out at night. They are one of the hairiest of all tarantulas, and they live in South America."

"So what's a South American pink-toe tarantula doing in my backyard?"

"I bet it escaped!" said Webster. "Tarantulas are super fast. They're

23

escape artists. One time my cousin was cleaning his tarantula's cage, and he left the screen at the top open just a crack. The tarantula got loose and was missing for a whole day."

"How did they find it?"

"They put out some crickets and it came out when it got hungry. His tarantula was just hiding—inside his sneaker!"

"Phew. Luckily my sneakers are too

stinky even for a tarantula," said Stink.

"Did you hear about the tarantula that went to college?" asked Webster.

"He liked to surf the web?" Stink asked.

Webster cracked up. "No. It's not a joke. This girl took her pet tarantula to college and it got loose in her dorm and crawled down three flights of stairs. They found it in the bathroom trying to climb into the toilet to get water."

"Yikes!" said Stink. "I'm never going to college now."

"Another time a lady was on a plane and she was watching a movie and she felt something crawl up her leg, and it was an escaped pet tarantula!"

"I'm never riding in a plane, either."

"Yep. You have arachnophobia."

"If that's fear of spiders, I've got it bad," said Stink.

"Just think," said Webster. "Maybe your pink-toe tarantula is somebody's pet. And it escaped and went on a wild adventure and ended up in your backyard."

"You're right," said Stink. "What if some kid took her tarantula to school and it escaped out of her backpack and climbed up into her hair and she stuck her head out the bus window and the spider got blown off and sailed through the air over houses and trees and roof-tops and *PA-LOP!* It landed right here on Croaker Road."

Webster's eyes were the size of mega marbles. *"¡Qué padre!"*

"Just saying," said Stink.

"We have to rescue it," said Webster. "Somebody around here is missing their pet. And if it is a pet, it might not be able to survive very long in the wild."

Stink had rescued guinea pigs. But they were cute and furry, not hairy and scary. "To rescue it we have to find it. It's kind of hard to look for something I don't really want to find because it gives me the heebie-jeebies."

"It might be hard to find. One acre of land can have up to one million spiders."

Gulp!

"Hey, maybe it's up in a tree," said Webster. "Pink-toes like to climb trees."

Stink was standing right under an oak tree. He imagined a giant pink-toe tarantula falling out of the tree and landing smack-dab on top of his head.

"AAAAAAGGGH!" Stink ran inside the house as fast as he could run.

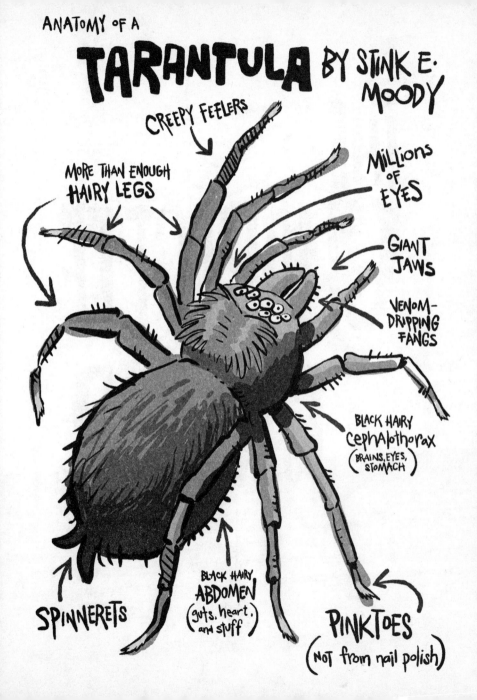

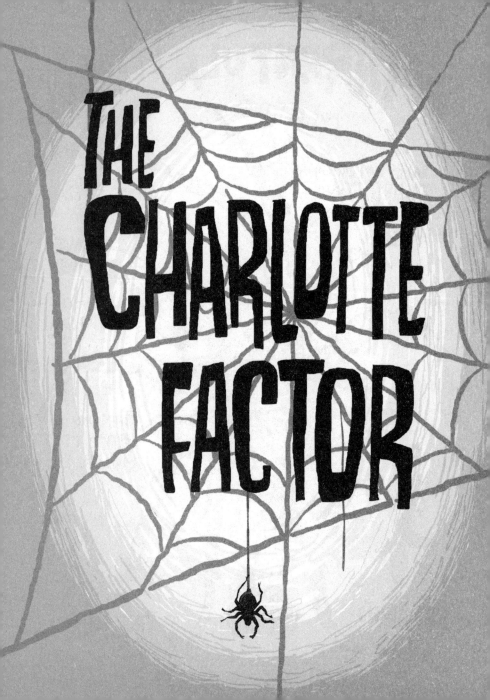

Webster ran after him. Stink shuddered just thinking about that spider. "Help! I gotta get over my arachno-thingy."

"Maybe I can talk you out of being afraid of spiders," said Webster. "You like facts. Let's start with some spider facts. Tarantulas are called hairy mygalomorphs. Sounds cool, right?"

"Sounds big and scary to me."

"They have fangs. And they have hairs with pokey things like cactus spines. If an owl or skunk threatens them, they can shoot hairs at them." Webster pretended to be attacked by a thousand tarantula hairs. "RAHHHH!"

"That's kinda cool," said Stink. "You sure know a lot about spiders."

"My name is *Web*-ster. Just call me the Web Man."

Stink grinned.

"Tarantulas are afraid of people, just like you're afraid of them," said Webster.

"Really?"

"In some countries, people eat fried tarantulas. My cousin says they're gooey like peanut butter and taste like crab cakes."

"Eww. Hairy peanut butter," said Stink. "What else you got, Web Man?"

"Spider blood is light blue, like raspberry ice-pops or puppy eyes. That's not scary." Webster scratched his head. "Are you cured yet?"

"Not yet," said Stink.

"Let's try the Charlotte Factor. Here's how it works. I'll read to you from *Charlotte's Web*. Charlotte is a good spider who tries to cheer up Wilbur the pig by writing kind words like *terrific* in her web. If you like reading about Charlotte, maybe you'll start to like spiders."

Webster read one whole entire chapter. "Are you cured yet?"

"Not yet."

Webster taught Stink how to sing "The Itsy-Bitsy Spider" in Spanish.

"Are you cured yet?" asked Webster.

"Not yet," said Stink.

"I'll tell you a spider joke!" said Webster. "Then spiders will seem funny, not scary. Why do spiders make good baseball players?"

"Why?" asked Stink.

"They catch flies!"

Stink cracked up.

"See? It's working!" said Webster. "What happened when the girl bit into a sandwich with a daddy longlegs in it?"

"It became a daddy short legs!" said Judy, popping into Stink's room.

"Hey, no spying on us," said Stink. "We're doing something."

"Maybe I want to do it, too," said Judy.

"You don't," said Stink.

"I'm helping Stink to get over his

arachnophobia," said Webster.

"Fear of spiders," said Stink.

"You can help," said Webster.

"No! She can't!" said Stink.

When Stink wasn't looking, Judy crossed her thumbs and wiggled her eight fingers in front of the desk lamp. "Stink! Look!" she cried.

Stink saw the shadow of a giant spider creepy-crawling across the wall.

"AARGH!" yelled Stink. He hopped up and ran around in circles.

"It's just Judy making hand shadows," said Webster.

"Out!" said Stink, pointing to the door.

"I was just trying to help," Judy said with a sly grin as she left the room.

"How about if you try looking at a picture of a spider?" Webster suggested.

"I have a book about spiders," said Stink. "But I hid it in my Shark Attack game because it creeps me out."

Webster went into the closet and pulled out the game with the *Big Head*

Book of Spiders. "We'll start small." He flipped through the pages.

"So. Many. Spiders." Stink flinched. He shielded his eyes.

"See this spider? The Samoan moss spider. It's the smallest spider in the world. It's only the size of a pencil point."

Stink the Science Nut perked up. A spider the size of a pencil point was interesting. A spider the size of a pencil point was fascinating. A spider the size of a pencil point was scientific!

41

He peered at the spider. "That's not so scary," said Stink.

"Have you ever heard of a rainbow-hued peacock spider? It's only as big as a fingernail. They can wave their rainbow-colored butts in the air and dance."

"Whoa. A dancing spider?" Stink peered closer at the picture.

Before you could say *hairy mygalomorph*, the science in Stink won out over the scared in him. Stink had his head in a book. Not just any book. A book about . . . hairy, scary spiders.

HOW to MAKE A SPIDER HAND SHADOW

 With your palms facing up, cross your left wrist over your right wrist.

 Lock your thumbs.

3 Spread your fingers to create eight legs.

4 Hold your hands in front of a flashlight to create the shadow!

CLOSE ENCOUNTERS OF THE SPIDER KIND

The itsy-bitsy spider climbed up the water-spout . . .

But the spider was NOT itsy-bitsy. The spider was not teensy-weensy. It was biggy-wiggy. Fangy-wangy. Hairy-scary! Freaky-deaky!

The monster-sized spider was all leggy. It inched its way down from the ceiling on a single silk thread. It hung right above . . . Stink's mouth!

Open wide and say "Ahh!" Stink's mouth was open. Wide open. Stink's mouth was stuck! H-E-L-P! He could not get his mouth to close.

Yikes! Stink E. Moody ate a spider! A biggy-wiggy, all-leggy monster spider.

Stink woke up. He threw off the covers. Spiders were creepy-crawling all over him! Stink squirmed. Stink itched. Stink scratched his spider bites.

Wait just a creepy-crawly second! Stink looked at both of his arms. Stink checked his legs. Stink lifted up his pajama top.

Phew! There weren't any real spiders

on him. He didn't really eat a monster spider. It had all been a dream. A bad dream. A nightmare.

A spider-mare!

Stink could no way, no how fall asleep now. There was a tree right outside his window. What if that pink-toed hairy beastie threw out some silk and swung from that tree and parachuted over to Stink's window and squeezed through a crack right into Stink's room and crawled into his race-car bed?

Stink hopped out of bed. He locked the window. He pulled the curtains shut. The house was quiet.

Clock-ticking quiet.

Stink got rid of all things spider.

He hid his spider ring in his desk drawer. He turned his Spiderman sleeping bag inside out. He put the *Big Head Book of Spiders* back inside his Shark Attack game. The spider plant by the window would have to live in the closet for tonight.

At last, his room was spider-free.

Stink crawled back into bed. He hugged his stuffed yeti and hunkered under the covers, all snug in his bed. But visions of fangs and spinnerets still danced in his head.

Next thing he knew, Stink was being attacked by a goliath bird-eating tarantula named Blondie. "I'm going to eat you alive, Shrimp!" said the tarantula.

"Not if I can help it, Blondie!"

Blondie rubbed her hind legs and made a hissing noise that sounded like pulling apart Velcro. The spider released a cloud of prickly hairs. "Take that, Porcupine," said Blondie.

Stink headed her off—*Zing! Zing! Zing!*—with his pool noodle. "You'll not make Swiss cheese out of me, Blondie." Blondie was just about to take a bite when . . .

Morning! Light poured through the crack in the curtains. Spider dreams gave Stink the heebie-jeebies. He took his pool noodle down to breakfast, just in case.

At the table, Stink folded origami cranes to take his mind off of spiders. "Mom, I need a dollar for lunch money."

"I just gave you two dollars yesterday," said Mom.

"I know," said Stink, "but I may have turned my extra dollar bill into an origami jumping frog, and it leapfrogged away from me."

"Stink, that frog is still out in the backyard somewhere," said Judy. "Go get it."

Stink glanced out the back window. "I'll do three things from your Chore Chart *and* you can keep the dollar if *you* go get it."

"Feed Mouse, clean litter box, take out recycling," said Judy.

"Done," said Stink. "Check Cootie Corner—that's where I last saw it."

Judy ran outside. She was gone a long time. When she came back, she had leaves in her hair and scratches on her arm and grass stains on her knees.

"Whoa. You look like you were attacked by Spiderzilla!" said Stink.

Judy grinned and held up the dollar-bill frog. "Dollarzilla!"

At school that day, Stink had spiders on the brain. He saw them crawling down the hall, up the classroom wall, in the bathroom stall. The hourglass in science lab reminded him of a black widow. The violin in the music room reminded him of a brown recluse. Riley Rottenberger's striped shirt reminded him of a zebra tarantula.

Stink stayed inside during recess. He folded an origami paper boat. He folded a fox face. He folded a shark face.

Webster, Sophie of the Elves, and Riley Rottenberger came to find him.

"Come out on the playground with us," said Webster. Sophie nodded.

"Did you get in trouble or something?" asked Riley.

"Or something," said Stink, imitating his sister Judy. He folded a ninja star.

He folded another ninja star, and then another. He gave one each to Webster, Sophie, and Riley.

"This isn't about spiders, is it?" asked Webster.

"There are bazillions of spiders out there. Quadrillions! Spiders are everywhere. You told me one acre of land can have up to one million spiders! If our playground is half an acre, that's half a million spiders!"

"I used to be scared of spiders," said Riley. "But now I pick them up in my bare hands."

"For real?" asked Stink.

"For real. If I even saw a spider I'd scream my head off."

"How did you get cured?" asked Stink.

"It took a while," said Riley. "I did it in baby steps. First, I just thought about spiders . . . on purpose . . . a lot."

"Done," said Stink. "Spiders are about the only thing I can think about since I found Spiderzilla in my yard!"

"Then I looked at pictures of spiders. Spiders in magazines, spiders in books, even spiders on the nature channel."

"We tried that," said Webster. "We also sang the Itsy-Bitsy Spider song and told spider jokes. Even the Charlotte Factor didn't work."

"Then it's time to touch a spider," said Riley. "It tricks your brain into thinking you're not afraid. It works for fear of blood, fear of snakes, and fear of dirt, too."

Stink made a horror face.

"I didn't touch a spider right away. I had to work up to it. First I touched it with a paintbrush. Then I touched it with a glove on. Then I touched it with my bare hands."

"Maybe you could try petting something hairy first," said Webster.

Stink reached inside his desk. "How about an Abe Lincoln beard from when I was Abe Lincoln?"

Riley nodded.

"And you always carry that fuzzy yeti in your backpack," said Sophie.

Stink closed his eyes. He stroked the Abe Lincoln beard. He petted the yeti. All of a sudden, he jumped up out of his seat and shook his head. "It feels creepy!"

"Okay, forget closing your eyes. We need something that looks more like a real spider to trick your brain. Something you can touch with your eyes open."

Sophie held up an origami bug. "What if you made an origami spider?"

"Yeah! Origami spiders look real," said Webster.

"That's it!" said Riley.

"Just one problem," said Stink. "Origami spiders are hard to make. They're Level Medium."

"Time to graduate to Level Medium," said Riley.

La araña pequeñita

("THE ITSY-BITSY SPIDER" in SPANISH)

La araña pequeñita
subió, subió, subió.
Vino la lluvia
y se la llevó.

Salió el sol
y todo lo secó.
Y la araña pequeñita
subió, subió, subió.

Webster came over after school. Stink took out two squares of origami paper. They stared at the directions for a long time.

"There are two halves to the spider: the head and the body. Each half has four legs. Which one do you want to make?" asked Stink.

"Head," said Webster.

Stink started his half with a frog base. Easy-peasy! He turned the paper top to bottom. He grabbed two flaps and pulled them apart. He made a mountain fold. He made a valley fold. He made an inside reverse fold.

Voilà! NOT!

"Something's not right," said Stink. "My half looks more like a four-legged pretzel!" Stink and Webster cracked up.

Webster started his half with a frog base. He made a valley fold.

66

He repeated the fold, just like the directions said. He turned it over. "My spider head looks like Darth Vader's helmet."

"Maybe if we put the two halves together it will look right," said Stink. He attached the Darth Vader head to the pretzel body.

Frankenspider!

Stink and Webster started over. They tried again. And again. They folded and refolded. They creased and double creased. They reverse folded and repeated.

Finally, Stink had four legs and a body. Webster had four legs and a head. Webster blew into the spider body. Poof! He inserted the spider head into the body.

At last! An eight-legged, not-creepy, origami tarantula.

"We did it!" said Webster. "We're the best."

"We climbed Level Medium and conquered it like Mount Everest," said Stink.

Webster took out a marker and colored the tarantula's toes pink.

"Freaky," said Stink. "It looks so real."

"It's just paper," said Webster. "Remember, you made it yourself. So it's not scary."

"It wasn't scary when it was a pretzel," said Stink. "But now it's a spider!"

Webster set the origami spider on Stink's desk. "How about if you start by staring at the spider for three minutes without looking away?"

Stink stared at the origami tarantula. He blinked. He blinked some more. But he did not look away.

"Good," said Webster. "Now I'm going to make it crawl on your shoe. Ready?"

"Ready," said Stink.

Webster made the paper tarantula crawl across Stink's stinky sneaker.

"I didn't even get a shiver!" said Stink.

"Next the tarantula will crawl up your leg to your knee."

"Check me out," said Stink.

"No problemo," said Webster. "Now the tarantula will crawl up your arm."

"Wait? What?"

Webster marched the origami tarantula up Stink's arm. "How's it feel?"

"I only got two shivers and three goose bumps!" said Stink. "Hand me the paintbrush."

Stink touched the origami tarantula with a paintbrush. He touched it while wearing a glove. He touched it with his bare hands!

"You did it!" said Webster. "Now let's go search for the real thing. Ready?"

"Ready," said Stink. "Operation Search-and-Rescue Pink-Toe Tarantula will begin in five, four, three, two, now!"

Webster headed for the door. Stink did not move. His feet were glued to the floor.

"What's wrong?" asked Webster.

"Maybe I should, um, touch just one more hairy thing with my eyes closed?"

"Okay, but that's all," said Webster.

"And one more hairy thing with my eyes open."

"And that's all?" asked Webster.

"Then make the origami spider crawl up my arm one last time."

"And that's all?"

"That's all," said Stink.

At last, it was time. Time to find that South American pink-toe tarantula.

"Ready or not, here we come," called Stink. He crept across the grass, slow as a snail, carrying a critter case and inching his way over to Cootie Corner.

"Come out, come out, wherever you are," called Webster. They searched in the tall grass and under piles of leaves.

They turned over rocks and crawled along the fence line on hands and knees.

"We're tarantula detectives," said Stink. "Our mission is to locate the suspect and return it to its rightful owner."

"We're super spies. Spider spies. You can't say *spi-der* without saying *spy.*"

"Look for something pink. And hairy," said Stink.

Webster kicked at the leaves. "I spy with my little eye . . . something pink!" He picked it up.

"Rats," said Stink. "Just an old sand-box shovel."

Holes had been dug here, there, and everywhere. "Are all these holes from when you were searching for a prehistoric saber-toothed cat tooth?" asked Webster.

"Yep," said Stink. "Hey! Maybe Lula is hiding in one of the saber-tooth holes."

"How do you know the spider's name is Lula?" Webster asked.

Stink shrugged. "I don't. I just thought she looked like a Lula."

Webster peered into each hole. Stink poked a stick inside one, then another. No Lula.

"We have to think like a tarantula," said Webster.

"If you were big and hairy, where would you hide?" asked Stink.

"Up in a tree?" said Webster.

Stink tapped the side of his head. "Smart thinking, Webster."

"Well, I am named after a diction-ary," said Webster. Stink cracked up.

Stink and Webster climbed the old oak in Cootie Corner. They looked up. They looked down. They looked all around.

"Hey, there's Judy," said Stink. "Hide!" Stink pulled a branch down in front of them and hid behind the leaves.

Judy ran over to the oak tree. "Stink. I know you're up there. I can see the leaves shaking."

"That's just a squirrel," said Stink.

"Squirrels don't talk, Stinkerdoodle. I came to tell you to come inside. Now. Mom and Dad said it's chore time, and you have to do my chores for me. Remember?"

"But we're being Super Spider Spies," said Stink. "Super Spider Spies don't do chores."

"If you don't do my chores, you're going to be up a tree for real. Get it?"

"Hardee-har-har," said Stink. He and Webster scrambled down out of the tree. "Sorry, Webster. I have double chores because I have to do Judy's. Long story."

"I can help," said Webster. "Then it will go twice as fast and we can keep looking for Lula."

"Don't forget to feed Mouse, clean the litter box, and take out the recycling," said Judy.

"I know, I know, I know," said Stink.

Webster followed Stink inside. They fed Mouse. They scooped poop out of the litter box. P.U.!

"Doing chores is even harder than being tarantula detectives," said Webster.

"And way more stinky," said Stink. "Thanks for helping."

Next they went out to the garage to get the recycling. "If you carry one bag, I'll take the other," said Stink. "Then we can search for Lula some more!"

Stink and Webster took the bags over to the big blue bin. They lifted them into the air. Stink was just about to dump his bag full of jars and papers and cardboard and cans when something moved.

Stink jabbed a finger at an old tuna-fish can. "Did you see what I saw?"

"If you saw something move, then I saw what you saw."

"What was it?" Stink stuck his head inside the blue bin.

"I think that tuna-fish can is alive," said Webster, pointing.

Stink reached to grab the can. He pulled it out of the bin. He turned it over.

"AARGH!" yelled Webster.

"AARGH!" yelled Stink, flinging the can to the ground.

The tuna-fish can moved. The tuna-fish can scurried across the yard. The tuna-fish can did push-ups. The tuna-fish can lifted itself up!

Out crawled a South American pink-toe tarantula named Lula.

SPIDERLOCK HOLMES

All the creepy-crawlies are hiding from the great detective Spiderlock Holmes. The reason why is no mystery: when Spiderlock Holmes finds a bug, he eats it! Can you find the eight tasty critters hidden in the picture?

Free at last! Lula started legging it across the backyard.

"Help! She's getting away!" yelled Stink.

Webster ran after her. "She's making a run for it. Hurry. Before she hides!"

Lula was fast. She was making a beeline for the Toad Pee Club tent. Webster pounced. Too late! "Oh, no!

Looks like she went under the tent."

Stink poked his head in. He watched a lump crawl along the tent floor.

"Try to catch her when she comes out the other side!" said Webster.

If he was going to rescue Lula, he had to do it . . . now.

"There she is!" yelled Webster. "Get her!"

Stink had to act fast. He did not stop to find a paintbrush. He did not stop to put on a glove. EEK! Stink chased after that tarantula and scooped it right up in his bare hands!

AAAARRRRGGGGHHHH!

Webster opened the lid to the critter case. Stink tossed the tarantula inside.

"Hallelujah!" said Webster.

"Halle-Lula!" said Stink.

"I can't believe you touched it!" said Webster.

"Me either!" said Stink.

"You just shook hands with a hairy, scary spider," said Webster. "You, Stink Moody, touched a tarantula. With your bare hands! *¡Qué fantástico!*"

"I have the Tarantula Touch now." Stink held up his hands. "I'm never washing my hands again. Call me Edward Spiderhands."

Webster picked up the critter case. "This hairy Houdini almost got recycled! We better get her some food and water, and take her inside where she'll be safe."

"Not in my room, though," said Stink. "Nah-uh. No, siree, bobcat tail! I might have touched a tarantula, but no way am I sleeping with one in the same room."

"You should keep it in the bathroom," said Webster. "My cousin turns on the shower till it's hot and steamy. That's how tarantulas like it."

In the bathroom, Stink turned on the hot water till the mirror got steamy. He set the critter case with the tarantula on the back of the toilet. He closed the door.

A little while later, Judy went down the hall to the bathroom. She opened the door.

"AARGH!" She tore out of the bathroom, screaming her head off.

Mom came running up the stairs to see what was the matter. She went into the bathroom.

"AARGH!" Mom came running out, too.

Dad raced up the stairs. "What's all

the screaming about?" Mom and Judy pointed to the bathroom.

Dad stepped into the bathroom.

"AARGH!" He came rushing out, too.

Stink and Webster came out into the hall. "What's wrong? You're not afraid of a little spider, are you?" Stink teased.

"F-f-first of all," Judy stuttered, "that thing is not little. Second of all, that thing is hairy!"

"It's a South American pink-toe," said Stink.

"I'm all for spiders," said Judy, "but that giant hairy thing could give a person a heart attack."

"I thought you weren't scared of spiders," said Stink.

"I'm not," said Judy, "but Mom and Dad might be. We have to think of them."

"You can't keep a tarantula, Stink," said Mom.

"Why not?" asked Stink.

"Because you're scared of spiders, Stinkerbell!" said Judy.

"Not anymore."

"We don't know how to care for it," said Mom.

"It's probably somebody's special

pet, Stink," said Dad. "I say we take it to Fur & Fangs, and see if they know anything about it."

"Dad's right," said Mom. "Somebody around here might be missing a South American pink-toe tarantula."

"Webster and I could go look for signs on telephone poles," said Stink. "Like 'Lost Dog' signs. If somebody lost their tarantula, maybe they put up a sign. Then we can contact the owner."

"Fine," said Mom. "I'm willing to give it one more day. But if you don't find the owner by tomorrow, it's got to go."

Stink and Webster raced to the corner. Signs were stapled up and down the pole. "Wow. Three 'Lost' signs and one 'Found,'" said Stink. They read the first sign.

LOST BIRD

GREEN-AND-YELLOW PARAKEET
GOES BY THE NAME OF BINGO
Can sing "PLOP! PLOP! FIZZ! FIZZ!"
Return to 123 Frog Pond Lane

"That's funny!" said Webster. "Check this one out."

Have you seen ME?
Orange-and-white tabby cat
Scratches furniture
Poops on rug
If found, do not return to 201 Ribbet Road

"They don't even want their cat back!" said Stink.

FOUND: PUPPY

GRAY AND BROWN, BLACK MARKINGS ON FACE NO TAGS NOT FRIENDLY, WILL SCRATCH

IF YOURS, CALL 555-8913

"Duh! Look at the picture. It's a raccoon, not a puppy!" Stink and Webster could not stop laughing.

"There's one more," said Webster.

LOST CRAB
MIGHT ANSWER To NAME oF FIDDLES
IF FOUND, $10 REWARD
FOR NOT EATING IT.
Call Tim 555-5678

"Lost bird, cat, crab, and one found puppy-raccoon, but NO spider," said Stink.

"Poor Lula. What if her owner doesn't even know she's missing?"

"I got it!" said Stink. "I'll make a 'Found' sign."

After Webster went home, Stink drew
a picture of Lula at the top of his sign.

FOUND

NOT SCARY

CUTE

PINK-TOE
TARANTULA

MAY ANSWER TO NAME OF LULA
FIND STINK AT 117 CROAKER ROAD

Stink ran to the corner and tacked
the sign on the pole.

105

That night he said, "Time for a bedtime story, Lula." He read that spider a chapter from *Charlotte's Web*. He told that spider a story about Anansi the Spider that he'd heard at the library. He sang Lula a lullaby—"The Itsy-Bitsy Spider" in Spanish—until he lulled that spider to sleep, even though it was nighttime and tarantulas are nocturnal.

At school the next day, it poured rain. Class 2D had indoor recess. Stink went up to his teacher's desk. "Mrs. D.," said Stink, "can I borrow a dollar?"

"Did you forget your lunch money, Stink?" asked Mrs. D.

"No. I'm not going to keep it. I'm going to make you a money tree. I'll give it right back. I promise."

"Money tree," said Mrs. D. "I like the sound of that." She took out a dollar bill and handed it to Stink.

"Thanks!" said Stink. Stink folded an origami dollar-bill tree. That's when he found a spider hiding on Mrs. D.'s dollar bill.

Stink showed his friends. He pointed to the corner of the dollar bill.

"That's not a spider, it's an owl," said Webster, squinting.

"Or an elf," said Sophie of the Elves.

"Nah-uh. That's a spiderweb. Owls do not live in spiderwebs. Neither do elves."

Stink could not wait to show his teacher. "Mrs. D., guess what I found on your dollar bill. A spider."

His teacher took out a magnifying glass and peered at the thing behind the number one on the dollar bill. "That does look a little like a spider," said Mrs. D. "I can't believe I've never noticed it before."

"Me either," said Stink.

"Are spiders a new interest, Stink? No more solar system? Shakespeare? Slime?"

"Brand new. A few days ago, I had arachnophobia. But I'm over it."

"Arachnids are interesting," said Mrs. D. "They've been around for more than five hundred million years."

Stink shivered. But it was not the fearful shiver of an arachnophobe. It was the shiver of excitement that came with learning a new scientific fact.

For the rest of the school day, Stink could not stop thinking about Lula.

Had anybody seen his sign? Did some-body come to get the lost spider? What if he never saw Lula again? Down came the rain and washed the spider out.

Stink splashed his way home from the bus and barged inside the front door. "Is Lula still here? Did anybody—"

"She's still here," said Mom. "You're dripping! Boots, Stink."

Stink yanked off his boots and his slicker. "So nobody came? She doesn't belong to anybody?"

"Stink, remember what we talked about," said Mom.

"But it's raining out. Can't we give my sign some more time? Lula's helping me to get over my arachnophobia."

"Our bathroom has serious spider cooties now," said Judy. "This morning I found a tarantula hair in my toothbrush. No lie."

Stink's eyes got wide. "Uh-huh," said Judy. "That means Lula got out and was wandering around in there— all over the bathroom."

Gulp!

"I think the rest of us are starting to catch arachnophobia," said Mom. "Put your boots back on, Stink. Dad said he'll take you to the pet shop."

When Stink got to Fur & Fangs, he looked for Mrs. Birdwistle. She was the owner of the world's best pet store and expert rescuer of one hundred and one guinea pigs.

Mrs. Birdwistle would know just-exactly-for-sure what to do about Lula. Stink found her feeding the Chinese water dragon in the reptile section.

"Stink! My favorite guinea-pig rescuer!" said Mrs. Birdwistle. "What brings you to Fur & Fangs? Do you need some dried crickets for Toady?"

"I found this in my backyard," said Stink, holding up the critter case. "It's a South American pink-toe tarantula and might be named Lula."

"Who's a naughty girl?" Mrs. Birdwistle said to the tarantula. "We should call you Houdini because you're such an escape artist."

"So . . . you know her?" Stink asked, rocking on his tiptoes.

"The owner comes in every day,

hoping somebody might find her pet tarantula. This is your lucky day, Stink Moody. She's here right now."

"Here?" asked Stink. "Now?"

"How about that," said Dad.

"She's in back with the red-knee tarantula," said Mrs. Birdwistle. "You are going to make somebody very happy today."

"Go ahead, Stink," said Dad. "I'll be right here looking at the parrots."

Stink carried Lula down the aisle past the ball python and the fancy corn snake. Past the black mollies and gold dust mollies. Past the fantail guppies and neon tetras. Past the emperor scorpion and the Costa Rican zebra tarantula.

A girl came running up to him. "My tarantula!" she shouted. "You found her! You found her! You're a lifesaver!"

Stink looked at the smiley girl with curly hair. "Wait a second. Don't I know you? You visit your dad sometimes in our neighborhood."

The girl held out her hand to shake. "Izzy Azumi, F.D.O. Future Dog Owner."

"Stink Moody, O.S.H. Official Spider

Handler." Stink held out the critter case. "Here's Lula. I bet you've been missing her."

"I missed her so much! But her name's Kiki. She's named after a Hawaiian superhero I like to draw. Kiki the Superbad wears a magic lei and springs off of her supersonic surfboard to fight one-eyed monsters. Her robot dog is always at her side."

"Kiki's a cool name," said Stink.

"I can't believe you found her!" said Izzy.

"It wasn't easy," said Stink. "She almost got recycled!"

"Yikes," said Izzy. "Don't tell my dad. See, Kiki's my practice pet."

"Your practice pet?" asked Stink.

"My dad promised I could get a dog at his house. But first he said I had to show him I could take care of a pet."

Dad came over and stood behind Stink.

"Everything was going great until I took Kiki out for a walk the other day. After her walk I put her back in the tank, but I must not have closed the lid tight and she got away. She's been missing for more than three days."

"So your dad won't let you get a dog

if you lost your practice pet?"

Izzy nodded. "A minute ago, F.D.O. almost stood for Failed Dog Owner. But maybe now my dad will let me. Thanks for finding her."

"Stink took good care of her," said Dad.

"I hope she's okay," said Stink. "She didn't eat today. And she keeps turning over on her back."

"Let's ask Mrs. Birdwistle to take a look," said Dad.

Izzy carried her tarantula over to Mrs. B. "Kiki's not moving," said Izzy. "And Stink says she turns over on her

back. Do you think she's okay?"

"I noticed she has a bald spot, too," said Dad.

Mrs. Birdwistle peered at the tarantula. "I think Stink found her just in time," said Mrs. B. "Don't worry. Kiki's fine. She's just getting ready to molt."

"She's going to shed her skin?" asked Stink. "Cool!" Izzy's eyes grew wide.

Mrs. Birdwistle told Izzy how to take care of Kiki while she was molting.

Before Stink could say *exoskeleton*, it was time to say goodbye.

Goodbye to Lula, the lost-and-found South American pink-toe tarantula with the superbad superhero name of Kiki.

When Stink got home, he was quiet. As quiet as a trapdoor spider waiting to catch a beetle. He slumped like a lump on the couch. Stink was down in the dumps.

"What's wrong with you, Stinkerbell?" Judy asked. Stink shrugged and dragged himself upstairs.

"Could he be missing that spider?" Mom asked.

"Maybe he has the opposite of arachnophobia," said Judy. "No-spider-itis."

Upstairs in his room, Stink put on his spider ring. He turned his Spiderman sleeping bag right side out. He rescued his *Big Head Book of Spiders* from inside his Shark Attack game. He freed his spider plant from the back of the closet.

He sang "The Itsy-Bitsy Spider" to Toady. Even that did not cheer him up.

Stink took a bath. He read one whole chapter of *Charlotte's Web*. But it just wasn't as much fun without Lula, aka Kiki the Superbad.

"Stink," called Judy up the stairs. "Come see what Mom and I did. It will cheer you up." Judy wiggled her toes. "We painted our toenails pink!"

"Actually, mine are called Ballet Slipper Beauty," said Mom, holding out a foot.

"Mine are called This Little Pinky, whatever that means," said Judy. "It's to remind you of the pink-toe tarantula. In case you feel sad or something."

"Thanks," said Stink. "That's funny."

"I could paint your nails, Stink." Judy held up a bottle of nail polish. "How about Cherry Berry Bubble

Gum? Or Flipped-Out Flamingo?"

"I'm good," said Stink.

"We could play double spider soli-
taire," said Mom.

"Or I could teach you how to dance
the tarantella," said Judy. "It's a step-
hop dance from Italy that makes you
look like you've been bitten by a spider."

"Thanks, but I have origami to fold." He folded a rainbow spider. He folded a two-headed spider. He folded a whole spider family until it was time for dinner.

The next morning, Stink hurried outside. He looked in the tall weeds and all around the yard and up in the old oak tree. But he did not find one creature. Not a house spider. Not a cricket. Not one worm.

Stink stuck his head in the recycling bin. He turned over a tuna-fish can. Not one single escaped South American pink-toe tarantula. Not even a zebra tarantula. Or a plain old curly-hair tarantula. BOR-ing!

When Stink popped up out of the bin, there she was, right smack-dab in the middle of his backyard!

Not Kiki the Tarantula, but Izzy Azumi herself. And she was turning a cartwheel. She looked like she had eight legs!

"Did you bring Kiki over?" Stink asked.

"Hi, Stink," said Izzy. "Your dad told me you were out here."

"Did you?" Stink asked again.

"Sorry. I can't move her or take her outside for a week. Because she molted!" Izzy held up a plastic bag. "I brought you something."

The something had eight legs. The something had an inside-out middle.

136

The something had no head. But the something looked just like a tarantula.

The something was a skeleton. An *exo*skeleton of a tarantula. Lula, aka Kiki, had shed her skin!

"Freaky-deaky," said Stink. "Wait till I show the Web Man. That's my friend Webster. This is the coolest thing ever. Are you sure I can keep it?"

"I'm sure. It's to thank you for taking care of Kiki."

"This is even better than my dried-up baby belly button that Judy took to school for Share and Tell." Izzy scrunched her nose. Stink cracked up.

Izzy turned another cartwheel. Judy came outside. "Hi, Izzy Azumi! Remember me? Judy Moody? You taught me how to do a cartwheel one time. Watch." Judy put her hands down flat, kicked her feet in the air and . . . fell on her rear.

"She looks like a Brazilian wandering spider doing a threat dance," said

Stink. "Am I right?" Izzy nodded.

"Did you know the goliath tarantula can eat a hummingbird?" asked Stink.

"Jumping spiders can jump more than fifty times their body length," said Izzy.

Izzy told Stink all about Kiki molting. And Stink taught Izzy how to sing "The Itsy-Bitsy Spider" in Spanish.

"I liked it better when you were afraid of spiders," said Judy.

Izzy stayed for dinner. "Did you know there are so many spiders in the world that they could eat all the humans on Earth in one year?" asked Stink.

"Is that true?" asked Judy.

"No lie," said Stink. "Spiders could eat all of us and still be hungry."

"The entire spider population on Earth weighs twenty-five million tons," said Izzy.

"Yeah, that's almost four hundred seventy-eight *Titanics*," said Stink.

"Kids," said Mom, "can we have one spider-free meal?"

"That means no exoskeletons on the table while we eat," said Dad.

"For the next twenty minutes," said Judy, "this is officially a Spider-Free Zone."

Stink munched on a taco shell. He checked the clock. The big hand hardly seemed to move. Nineteen more minutes to go. "Did you know Izzy has letters after her name? Izzy Azumi, F.D.O."

"Future Dog Owner," said Izzy.

"Do you think you'll get a dog

141

anytime soon?" Judy asked.

"I hope so. Now that Stink rescued my spi—oops, I mean, pet."

Stink checked the clock again. "Do you think that clock is broken?"

"It works," said Mom.

"It works," said Dad.

"For now," said Stink, "you can be Izzy Azumi, P.T.T.O. Pink-Toe Tarantula Owner!" Izzy beamed, showing off a missing tooth.

Judy shot Stink a sourball look. "What?" said Stink. "I didn't say *spider*. I said *tarantula*."

"Same-same," said Judy.

"I only said *spider* to tell you I didn't say *spider*," Stink explained.

"You said it two more times!" Izzy giggled.

"Twenty minutes feels like three hours," said Stink.

"It's hard to believe a few days ago this kid was terrified of spiders," said Dad.

Mom nodded. "Now he can't go twenty minutes without talking spiders."

"Time's up!" said Stink, bouncing in his chair. "I can't wait until March fourteenth!"

"Me too!" said Izzy.

"March fourteenth?" said Dad. "National Pi Day?"

"National Bake-a-Pie Day?" asked Mom. "Or is it National Potato Chip Day?"

Judy flipped pages on the wall calendar to March 14. "National Genius Day? Ask a Question Day? Nothing about spiders here. Oh, wait—"

"National Save a Spider Day!" Izzy squealed.

"On March fourteenth, Izzy Azumi and I are going to save a spider."

"Maybe it will be a dark-footed ant spider," said Izzy. "A tricky spider that looks like an ant!"

"Maybe it will be a spider species that hasn't even been discovered yet!"

Just then, Izzy's dad tooted the horn out front. It was time for her to go.

"Say hi to Kiki for me," said Stink. "Remember to read her a bedtime story. And don't forget to sing 'The Itsy-Bitsy Spider' to her."

"Come see Kiki next week." Izzy waved goodbye. "Remember, Stink, you are always within three feet of a spider."

Stink sat in the dark, under the Red Spider Nebula at the center of the Milky Way. He felt a shiver. Not a shiver of fear. Not a shiver of cold. A shiver of wonder at the Earth. A shiver of awe at the universe, with its many creatures.

Suddenly Stink felt a little less alone. After all, there were about twenty-one quadrillion spiders in the world. Spiders were all around.

Freaky-deaky!